Day Care Days

by **Mary Brigid Barrett**   Illustrated by **Patti Beling Murphy**

Little, Brown and Company
Boston New York London

The alarm rings — BRRRRING!!!
Baby cries.
Daddy blinks his bleary eyes.
Mommy jumps up out of bed,
Kisses Sister on the head.

Quick, go potty!
Daddy shaves.
Mommy, in the shower, waves.
Sister, SWISH-SWISH, brushes teeth.
Baby's diaper starts to leak!

Pull on pants, then a shirt.
Head gets stuck. OUCH, that hurt!
Daddy ties the big-boy shoes.
Baby toddles in and coos.

Out the door,
And in the car.
But the car does not go far.
Right back home. Get Old Bear.
Old Bear must go everywhere.

Drop off Mommy
At the train.
Sister goes to school again.
To the day care off we go,
Sun or rain or sleet or snow.

Here we are.
Baby, too.
I hug Dad good-bye, so blue.
Daddy kisses tears away.
He'll be back at the end of the day.

Coats in cubbies,
Toys from the bin,
Free playtime till everyone's in!

Stack up the blocks, put away the rings.
Stand in a circle, everyone sings!

Grab coats and mittens,
Run out to play —
Swing high, swing low, swing up, up, and away!

SWOOSH down the slide! ZOOM! Be a plane!
Quick, inside — it's starting to rain.

Backpacks out.
It's time for lunch.
Goodies from home. MUNCH, MUNCH, MUNCH!

Pillow and mat, snuggle down for a nap.
Wake up soon, with a clap, clap, clap!

Paint shirt on.
Brush in hand.
Paint a zany zigzag land.

Paint on hair, paint on the nose.
Paint on hands, and elbows, and toes.

Clean up for snack:
Cookies to eat,
With milk or juice, a special treat!

Story-time book, adventures galore.
Hug Old Bear and sprawl on the floor.

Rosie goes home,
And Willy, too.
And Emmie and Pat and Lizzy and Drew.
Sit all alone with modeling clay,
Hoping Daddy is on his way.

Daddy is here!
He's at the door!
Baby jumps up from the floor!
Outside, the rain falls, SPLITTER-SPLAT.
Grab Old Bear, and boots and hat.

Home we go,
Into the tub,
Warm water bubbles and scrub, scrub, scrub.

Into pajamas. Daddy starts to cook.
Sis shows Mom her library book.

Dinnertime.
Then up the stairs.
Brushing teeth and combing hair.

Snuggle deep down into bed,
Touching Old Bear, head to head.
Daddy hugs me,
Says he's proud,
Calls, "I love you" right out loud.

Mom kisses me, turns out the lights,
And whisper-sings a sweet "Good night."

For Elizabeth, Emily, and Patrick,
with great love and abiding affection

— Mom

For Shaun, Hanni, Piza, and Posey

— P. B. M.

Text copyright © 1999 by Mary Brigid Barrett Groth
Illustrations copyright © 1999 by Patti Beling Murphy

First Edition

Library of Congress Cataloging-in-Publication Data

Barrett, Mary Brigid.
  Day care days / by Mary Brigid Barrett ; illustrated by Patti Beling Murphy. — 1st ed.
  p. cm.
  Summary: A little boy recounts the events of his family's busy day, from waking up,
getting dressed and off to day care, until his daddy picks him and his baby brother up
and brings them home.
  ISBN 0-316-08456-5
  [1. Family life — Fiction. 2. Day care centers — Fiction. 3. Stories in rhyme.]
  I. Murphy, Patti Beling, ill. II. Title.
  PZ8.3.B25275Day 1999
  [E] — dc21   97-52105

10 9 8 7 6 5 4 3 2 1

SC

Printed in Hong Kong

The paintings for this book were done in gouache on watercolor paper.
The text was set in Shannon Bold, and the display type is Agenda Bold.